Stories of Regional America—some humorous, some filled with pathos—spotlight both the likes and differences of special peoples in colorful places. These peoples form the melting pot, which has become America. The action-filled accounts, each based on true fact, give the reader a deeper appreciation of his cultural background and a greater understanding of the peoples who have made his heritage possible.

Abe Lincoln and the River Robbers

BY LaVERE ANDERSON

ILLUSTRATED BY CARY

GARRARD PUBLISHING COMPANY
CHAMPAIGN, ILLINOIS

For
Patrick Scott Parker,
a fine boy

Contents

1. Abe Gets His Chance

Abe Lincoln hurried down the forest trail, a wide grin on his face. He had news—big news—and he could scarcely wait to get home and tell it.

Abe was nineteen years old in that spring of 1828, and so tall that he had to duck to get through doors. Now his long legs made quick work of the miles through the Indiana wilderness

6

to the one-room log cabin where the Lincolns lived.

He burst through the cabin door so fast that he almost forgot to duck. His parents were sitting before the fire.

"Mammy! Pappy!" he cried. "I've got my chance to travel and see a piece of the world! Mr. James Gentry over at Gentryville has hired me to help take a boatload of farm produce all the way to New Orleans!"

Abe's mother looked at him anxiously. She knew that prosperous farmers sometimes loaded their surplus crops onto flatboats and floated them down the Ohio and Mississippi rivers to the New Orleans markets. She also knew that sometimes a boat and crew left for that long trip and were never heard from again.

"Rivers are dangerous, Abe," she said. "There be quick storms and shifty currents, and river pirates who'll rob and kill a man for no more profit than a side of pork. I'm afraid for you, Abe."

"But I won't be alone," Abe explained. "Mr. Gentry's son, Allen, is going too. He's a smart young fellow, and he's made the trip once before with his pa. We'll have a fine time."

"How much will Gentry pay you?" asked Mr. Lincoln. He was very poor, and what Abe earned helped to support the family.

"Eight dollars a month," said Abe proudly. "It will take three months to build a boat, to make the trip, and to come home. I'll earn $24, Pappy."

Mr. Lincoln nodded. "Gentry owns a string of farms and a boat landing on the Ohio River. He can afford it. You go, Abe. We need the money."

His mother rumpled Abe's thick black hair. "Go, and have that fine time," she said. "But be careful, Abe, be mighty careful."

Abe and Allen began building their flatboat on the bank of the nearby Ohio. They felled and trimmed oak trees in the forest and used Mr. Gentry's horses to drag the logs to the riverbank.

There they chopped and sawed the logs into planks. With a drawknife—a long knife with a handle at each end—they shaved the planks

8

smooth. They fastened the bottoms and sides of the boat together with wooden pegs and filled the seams with a stringy rope fiber called oakum to make the craft watertight. They built a deck shelter six feet high.

Then at the bow end of the boat they put a pair of long oars called bow sweeps, or "gougers," and at the stern a setting pole for steering that was called a stern sweep.

Abe was good at the work. His father was a carpenter and Abe had often helped him build cabins. Building a boat was more fun. Abe worked from daylight to dusk every day.

"Don't know as I'd be in such a hurry to finish that boat, Abe," said a young backwoods boy. He was one of a group who gathered on the bank each day to watch. "I been hearing there's strange things in that ole Mississip'. There's catfish so big that if a fellow falls overboard, they swallow him in one gulp."

"An' keep your eyes skinned for those half-horse half-alligator men, Abe," warned another lad. "Pa says they're thicker on the river than black bugs in spoiled bacon, an' there's nothin' they like better'n a fight. They'll bite off your nose for pure pleasure."

Abe's gray eyes twinkled. "I'll remember that, Bud," he promised, "and if I see one of them coming, I'll take off my nose and put it in my pocket."

In a few weeks the flatboat was finished, a rough but sturdy craft.

Mr. Gentry helped the boys load it with sides of bacon and venison hams, great sacks of shelled corn and cornmeal, barrels of apples and potatoes and other farm produce.

"Take good care of that cargo, boys," he told them. "It'll be worth a thousand dollars in New Orleans. Abe, you're a strong, sensible fellow, and I'm counting on you to stand by Allen if trouble comes."

"I will," Abe promised.

At last all was ready. On a bright, breezy morning the boys stood on the dock and told their families good-bye. Then they pushed out into the river. Allen was at a bow sweep, his brown hair blowing, his face red with excitement. Abe handled the big stern sweep.

The flatboat moved toward mid-channel, slowly at first, then more swiftly until at last the current caught it. The big boat straightened and headed downstream. Soon the boys could no longer see the people waving from the riverbank.

"Whee!" cried Allen. "We're on our way at last!"

It was a long, lazy day. The river carried them gently. The water sparkled in the sunshine, and along the banks the maples and hickories were touched with the first faint green of spring. Iroquois Indians had named the river "Ohio," a word that meant "the beautiful," and beautiful it was.

That night the boys tied up to a tree on the bank and slept on deck under the stars. In the morning they fried their breakfast of pork and cornmeal cakes in a fireplace made of a box filled with sand. Then they pushed off again.

Sometimes they poled. Sometimes they drifted. Sometimes Allen sat at an oar while Abe cooked a meal, and other times Abe took an oar while Allen washed their shirts over the side of the boat. Often they met other river traffic—

flatboats, keelboats rowed by singing men, glossy steamboats. "Howdy," the boys called across the water.

So the first days passed.

"I'm beginning to feel lazy," Abe said one afternoon. "Nothing to do but ride while the river does all the work."

Allen yawned and stood up to stretch. He was a head shorter than Abe, but strong like most backwoods boys. "I feel lazy too."

An hour later the wind arose and blew fiercely enough to whip the water into white-capped waves. The boat began to turn and twist.

Abe flung himself on the stern sweep.

"Grab a gouger," he shouted to Allen.

Straining at the sweeps, the boys tried to hold course, but the flatboat was hard to steer. Dark clouds formed overhead. Lightning forked the sky. A cold rain beat down, lashing boat and boys and almost blotting out the shoreline.

"We'd better head for land," yelled Abe above the crash of thunder as he struggled with the big sweep. "Hey—looky yonder. I can make out a houseboat on the left bank."

"Let's aim for it," Allen shouted back. "I'd feel better with some folks around tonight."

They fought every inch of the way through a river turned into a churning fury. The big boat tossed and bucked, twisted sideways, groaned as if it were a living thing in pain.

Yet inch by inch they neared the bank, and finally pulled into a clump of willows a stone's throw from the houseboat. From what little they could see in the blinding storm, it stood lonely and bleak, half on land and half sagging into the water.

Too wet and tired to investigate, the boys tied their boat to a willow tree, then crawled into their deck shelter and fell into an exhausted sleep.

During the night the storm passed. Morning dawned soft and blue. In the clear light the boys saw that it was not a houseboat they had for a neighbor. It was a flatboat like their own. Its wood still looked new, but the boat was rammed on the bank and broken into splintered pieces.

"Somebody had a bad time," Abe said gravely. "I hope they weren't hurt and could salvage

their cargo." Both boys knew it was more likely that bodies and cargo had floated downriver, leaving only the wrecked boat behind.

Soberly they pushed out into the stream. After a while Allen said, "Last night—we could have ended up like that other boat."

Abe nodded. "It's a mighty muscular river," he said, "and no place to get lazy."

2. The Pirate Den

"Hey, Abe, we've got company!" Allen said a few mornings later as they drifted smoothly down the Ohio. Abe took another bite from his apple and looked toward the boat's stern. An old man in worn clothes sat in a small scow alongside the flatboat, a fishing pole in his hand.

"Howdy, young fellers," he greeted them. "How about askin' me aboard to visit?"

"We'd better not," Allen whispered to Abe. "We're getting close to Cave-in-Rock, the old pirates' den. This may be a trick to rob us."

Abe studied the man. "One old fellow against two huskies like us, what could he do? If it's a trick, I'd like to see how he plans to work it. We'll keep our eyes peeled."

"All right." Allen motioned, and the old man tied his scow to the back of the flatboat and climbed nimbly aboard.

"Name's River Pete," he told them. "Had a mind to sit with you a spell. Gets lonesome on the river."

"Come sit," Abe invited, "and have an apple."

River Pete let out a high cackle of laughter as he took an apple from the tin plate. "By cracky, ever'where I go I get reminded of old Johnny Appleseed!"

"Who's that?" Allen asked.

"I don't rightly know his proper name," their guest said. "Ever'body just called him Johnny Appleseed. I used to see him often back in the old days, when he was trampin' all over the Ohio and Indiana wilderness plantin' appleseeds. Got 'em free from a cider mill up in Pennsylvania, and carried 'em around in leather bags. Showed farmers how to plant 'em and grow orchards. Why, Johnny brought bags of appleseeds right down this river in a canoe."

"Must have made a heap of money," Allen said.

"Nah," River Pete scoffed. "Never charged anybody a cent. Johnny never needed money. Lived off roots and berries he found in the woods, and what some farmer's wife would give him. Wore a coffee sack with armholes cut in it and went barefoot pretty near the whole year."

River Pete tossed his apple core overboard and took another apple. "Some folks laughed at old Johnny but most folks loved him, and the little children had good nourishin' apples because of him."

Abruptly he changed the subject. "Where you young fellers goin'?"

"New Orleans," said Allen.

"That's what I figured. You got a big cargo in that deck shelter. I can tell by the way your boat sits in the water. Got lots of meat and farm stuff?"

Allen nodded, suspicion flaring in his eyes.

"I know where you can sell some of it," River Pete declared. "Right down here a piece is a big cave where some folks live who are clean out of supplies. You pull in there and you'll sell a heap."

20

Abe had been watching the old man closely. "Reckon you mean Cave-in-Rock," he said. "A den of thieves."

"Yep, it used to be," River Pete agreed. "But not any more. Good people there now, lookin' for farms to settle. Just pull in and holler. They'll be mighty glad to see you."

Allen's face flushed with anger. He was ready to accuse the old man of trying to send them ashore so they could be robbed, but Abe shook his head warningly.

"We've got food to sell, all right," Abe told the riverman. "These people would be willing to pay good prices, I reckon."

"The best." River Pete threw his apple core overboard and reached for the tin plate again. "A clever parcel of fellers like you can make yourselves some money."

Suddenly he stood up. "Thanks for lettin' me sit and chin. Remember, just pull in by the cave and holler." Spryly he clambered down to his scow, untied the hitch rope, and rowed away.

"That old buzzard!" Allen exploded indignantly. "He was trying to send us to what would

probably be our deaths. That's an old trick to lure boatmen ashore. Why didn't you let me tell him we weren't as big fools as he thought?"

"It could be a trick," Abe said slowly, "and he thought a pair of country boys like us wouldn't know any better. Then again, he could have been honest. If he was, it wouldn't have been right for us to call him otherwise. But I reckon we won't stop at the cave to find out."

Soon the cliffs of Cave-in-Rock came into view.

The cave was a huge one, the boys knew. In earlier years, bands of outlaws living there had

been the terror of the river. When lawmen finally drove them away, 60 human skeletons were found back in the far reaches of the cave, and many more unlucky boatmen had been murdered and thrown into the water. Now nobody knew just who was living in the cave, but rivermen were still afraid of it.

"Looky yonder!" Abe said. "There must be six or eight fellows on the bank watching us."

As the flatboat came abreast of the cave entrance, the men on shore motioned for the boys to come in.

"Looks like they're waving paper money," Allen said. "Pretending they want to buy from us."

"Sorry, fellows, but we can't stop now," Abe called across the water. They swept past the entrance, the flatboat making good time in the strong current.

"Abe! Three of them are climbing into a skiff!" Allen cried. "They're coming after us!"

"Get to a gouger!" Abe said quickly.

Allen grabbed one bow sweep and Abe the other. Hard as they could, they pulled on the big oars and the flatboat spurted ahead. Behind them came the men in the skiff, gaining on them in the smaller boat. The chase was on.

"Faster!" Allen cried. "We've got to go faster!"

"Save your breath for rowing," Abe advised.

Grimly the boys bent to the sweeps. Muscles stood out like ropes on their backs. Sweat ran down their bodies. For minutes, as they labored, they saw nothing, heard nothing except the water splashing. Then Abe risked a backward glance.

"We're out-running them!" he shouted joyously. Then, "Allen, they've given up! They've stopped and are shaking their fists at us!"

The tired youths laid down their sweeps.

"Why did they quit?" Allen asked. "They could have caught us."

Abe pointed at the sky ahead where a ribbon of black smoke drifted. "A steamboat's coming around the point. They must have seen the smoke. They knew they couldn't board and fight us with a steamboat going past."

"We were lucky," Allen said. "They sure meant trouble."

From downstream came the steamboat—a graceful packet making her way up the wide, blue river.

"Prettiest boat I ever saw," Allen said fervently. "She saved our lives. She sure did save—Abe, why are you grinning?"

Abe grinned even more. "I was thinking that River Pete tricked us after all. He managed to talk about Johnny Appleseed long enough to eat three of our apples!"

3. Half-Horse and Half-Alligator

As the days passed, Abe and Allen began to feel like real rivermen. They caught silvery bass and had fish suppers. At night they camped on sandbars or tied up at riverfront towns. Abe learned a song from passing keelboatmen, and he sang it often and loudly in his raspy voice:

Hi-O, away we go
Floating down the river on the O-hi-o . . .

"Land o' Goshen, Abe!" Allen protested good-naturedly. "Won't you ever stop singing that song!"

"I'll stop when we get to the Mississippi," Abe promised.

At last they came to Cairo, Illinois, where the clear waters of the Ohio met the muddy Mississippi—the Great River, as the Indians called it. Often it was more than a mile wide.

Here the current was faster than on the Ohio. When all went well the boys traveled four or five miles an hour. But the Mississippi was treacherous. Sudden storms whipped up high waves that poured over the deck and threatened to upset the boat. The boys had to be constantly on guard for hidden snags in the riverbed or unexpected sandbars that could ground the craft. The wild river churned with whirlpools and eddies. If the boat was sucked into an eddy, it spun around until Abe and Allen, using all their brawn, could pull it out.

Although dangers came suddenly, they usually ended quickly. Most days were long and peaceful.

Abe marveled at all the strange new things he saw, for river traffic was heavy. The Mississippi was like a great avenue on which northern farmers, fur trappers, and lumbermen sent their goods south to the market of New Orleans, and southern planters sent their cotton, sugar, and tobacco northward.

There were rafts and canoes, barges, and clumsy boats called arks. There were steamboats glistening with white paint and red or blue trim. One day the boys saw a string of six flatboats tied one behind another.

A family lived on the first boat. The boys watched while a woman hung clothes on a line and children played on deck. Next came flatboats filled with farm produce, and next a boat where men were butchering hogs. The last boat was a "store" filled with tinware, tools, wagons, and plows to be sold at little river ports.

"People tie their boats together like that for company," Allen explained.

One evening, in the last moments of sunset, they stopped at Memphis, Tennessee. It was a settlement of 500 people.

"Memphis is called 'Flatboat Town,'" Allen remarked.

Abe could see why. There were so many flatboats clustered at the water's edge that the boys

had to tie to a boat far out and walk across six others to reach land. As they stepped ashore, they heard a loud voice boasting:

"I can outrun, outhop, outjump, throw down, drag out, and lick any man in the country. I'm half-horse and half-alligator, and I'm chock-full of fight!"

The voice belonged to a large, fierce-looking man who was stomping angrily up and down the beach. He had a black patch over one eye, and a shaggy black beard.

"What's the trouble?" Abe asked a group of flatboatmen.

"Same trouble we always have when a keel-boat stops here," a flatter snorted. "Keelboaters claim they're the kings of the river, and they're always wanting to crack a few heads to prove it. Cap'n Bob, there, is spoiling for a fight, but don't oblige him. He fights mean—gouges eyes and chews thumbs and butts you with his head."

"That's not polite fighting," Abe agreed. However, to Abe's way of thinking, the keelboatmen *were* the kings of the river.

Flatboats were floated downriver and then sold

in New Orleans for their lumber. They were one-way craft, and flatboatmen had to walk or take a steamboat home. Keelboats were not only floated downstream, they were rowed back up river by crews of 20 or more husky men who had to fight the current every inch of the way. Keelboats were much larger than flatboats, too. They were heavy and awkward to handle. To work on a keelboat was so hard and dangerous that any men who could take such a boat and its load of cargo up the powerful Mississippi really had to be half-horse and half-alligator.

Cap'n Bob was shouting again:

"I'm a rip-tailed roarer all the way from Salt Fork on Buzzard Run, and I can lick my weight in wildcats with my bare teeth while handcuffed. Maybe you never heard of the time the horse kicked me and put both his hips out of joint. If that's not true, cut me up for catfish bait. I'm going to live forever and then turn into a white-oak post. Who wants to fight me?"

He glared at the flatboatmen, but nobody volunteered.

Angrily he puffed out his chest, jumped up

in the air, and knocked his heels together. He looked so comical that Abe began to grin. Cap'n Bob saw him. Blood in his one good eye, the keelboater roared up to Abe. "You laughing at me, stranger?" he demanded.

Abe's grin grew wider. Folks said Abe could grin the bark off a tree. "I'm just a country boy out seeing the sights," Abe said, "and you're sure a sight to see, mister."

For a moment Cap'n Bob looked unsure

whether Abe had insulted or complimented him. Abe's friendly grin decided him. He swung around to the flatboatmen.

"Hear that?" Cap'n Bob shouted. "I'm a sight! That's what the stranger said and he's big enough to back up his words. Yessiree, I'm a rough, tough snorter and a snapping turtle and a sight! Anybody here want to say different?"

Nobody did. Cap'n Bob gave the flatters a disgusted look, then stomped away followed by his keelboat crew. At the water's edge he turned and favored Abe with a grin almost as wide as Abe's own. It was plain that Cap'n Bob enjoyed being a sight.

Back on their boat, Abe and Allen had begun to make cornbread for supper when a thin, ragged boy hopped onto their deck.

"Bennie, you come back here. We've got to move out," a man shouted at the lad from a nearby flatboat.

"Yes, Pa," the boy called. Then he turned to Abe and Allen. "You got any chewing tobacco?" he asked, his brown eyes anxious. "I don't mean to be begging, but I sure do need a chew."

Abe shook his head. "You're a little young for tobacco, aren't you?"

"I'm eleven," the boy said, "but it's not for me. It's for Old Al. Pa says we've got to go on downriver tonight, 'cause we're loaded with pork that wasn't cured proper and Pa's afraid it'll spoil if we don't get it to New Orleans fast. But I'm scared to travel at night if there's fog on the river. Fog fairly raises my hair!"

"Who's Old Al? Your pa?" Allen asked.

The boy looked surprised. "I thought everybody knew Old Al. He's a monster alligator with a golden crown who lives in the Mississippi, and when he smokes his pipe it makes fog on the river. But if you throw some chewing tobacco into the water, he gets so busy chewing he forgets to smoke."

Allen laughed. "Where'd you read that yarn?"

"I can't read," the boy said, "but everybody knows that fog is the smoke from Old Al's pipe."

He hopped onto another boat, and another, asking his question. Abe saw him disappear into the keelboat. Shortly he came skipping back, a big brown plug of tobacco in his hand.

"Cap'n Bob gave it to me," he shouted as he passed. "Cap'n Bob says he can chew more tobacco and spit less than any man in the land. I'll bet he can, too." Then the boy was gone, clutching his brown treasure.

In a short while Abe saw Bennie's boat leave port. Later the keelboat also moved out onto a river dyed lavender by the twilight. As they reached midstream, the keelboatmen began to sing:

Row, boys, row!
That's the way we go
All the way to Shawneetown
So row, boys, row.

Abe stood watching until the boat was lost in the purple shadows of evening, but still the brave song rang back across the water:

Hard upon the beach oar!
She moves too slow.
All the way to Shawneetown
Long time ago . . .

Abe thought he had never seen a more beautiful evening nor heard sweeter music. They brought a mist to his eyes and a catch to his throat.

"I hope Bennie's tobacco works," he said softly. "I hope there's no fog on the river tonight, and the pork doesn't spoil, and Cap'n Bob makes it safe to Shawneetown."

4. A Steamboat Race

Now the days grew warmer as they moved farther south. Along the shores the hickories and maples of the north had been replaced by magnolia and live oak trees strung with gray streamers of Spanish moss. Long-legged blue heron stalked the beaches. There were great plantations with white-pillared houses and fine lawns that stretched down to the river's edge.

"That's a mighty big cabin!" Abe said admiringly of one mansion. "But where do they get enough people to fill it?"

"They give parties." There was a twinkle in Allen's eyes. "I'll tell you a true story that I heard on my last trip.

"A flatboatman was drifting down this river one night, and he passed one of these houses all lighted up. There were a lot of people dancing to a plantation orchestra. Half an hour later he passed another house all lighted up and having a party. Later he passed another with a party going on, and then another. It was like that all night long.

"'Well,' he said to himself, 'this is the beatingest country for frolicking I ever saw. The whole river is one big jubilee!'

"Morning came, and then he found that he had got into an eddy. All night he'd been traveling around and around in a circle, and every half hour he'd passed the same house!"

Abe laughed. "That must have been a granddaddy eddy."

"Some eddies are as much as two miles around the outside," Allen said. "Hope we don't meet any of them."

One afternoon they saw heavy black smoke in the sky ahead. Then a steamboat came around the bend a half mile away. Showers of sparks poured from her two tall chimneys.

40

"Look at all that smoke!" Allen exclaimed. "You'd think she was in a race!"

"She is," Abe said, for around the bend came a second steamboat. Her smokestacks spurted flame.

"I'm glad the river is so wide here. I'd hate to be out there where they could run us down," Allen said. "Golly, the second one is catching up to the first."

On came the boats, their giant paddlewheels churning the water into foam. The decks of both boats were crowded with passengers who yelled and hooted at one another in friendly rivalry.

Abe sniffed the air. "Smells like somebody is frying bacon," he said in surprise.

"The firemen are throwing lard and bacon slabs and probably whole hams into the furnaces," Allen explained. "I saw it happen last trip. Fat makes a hotter fire than wood."

Abe frowned. He knew that in a boat powered by steam, the hotter fire made more steam and more steam made faster speed possible. Still, he didn't like the idea of wasting food. Since two steamboats would race almost any time they met,

a lot of lard, ham, and bacon must be wasted.

Now the racers were almost abreast of the flatboat. As they passed, Abe read their names painted on the big paddlewheel boxes. *Delta Rose* was in the lead and moving swiftly upstream, but the *Yazoo* was closing fast. The Mississippi continued to carry the boys downriver, but still they watched the race.

"*Yazoo*'s going to pass!" Allen cried. His face grew pink with excitement. "She *is* passing! Hooray for *Yazoo*! Hooray—OH, ABE!"

A thunderous explosion had split the air. From the *Yazoo* a great fountain of fire leaped skyward. Pieces of burning wood and red-hot metal flew from the *Yazoo* and struck the water, sizzling as they hit. The boys saw men and women jump overboard into the river and heard the screams of the injured rise piercingly above the roar of flames.

"The boiler exploded," Allen gasped. "Oh, those poor people."

The boys stared helplessly at the tragic scene, but there was nothing they could do. Their flatboat had already drifted beyond the racers.

They could not turn their heavy craft and row it upstream.

"The *Delta Rose* has stopped," Abe said at last. "She'll go back and pick up survivors."

Soon the flatboat rounded the bend. The boys could no longer see the burning steamboat, only a great cloud of oily smoke.

"Why did it happen?" Allen asked sadly. "They were just having fun. Everybody likes to race."

"I guess they overheated the boiler." Abe's voice was filled with pity. "They built up too much steam and the boiler couldn't hold it. I've heard of a lot of races that ended like this. I don't understand why people do it."

"But they were just having fun," Allen repeated. "Nobody meant any harm."

Then for a long time the two boys sat in silence and watched the dark cloud that streaked the sky.

5. Battle in the Dark

"Looks like we're going to get your pa's cargo safe to market after all. There were times back up the river when I didn't feel too sure of it," Abe told Allen one day.

They were passing the lively city of Natchez, Mississippi, where good citizens lived on the bluff high over the river and rowdy folk lived along the waterfront in Natchez-under-the-Hill.

When boatmen passed Natchez, they felt that the worst of their trip was over, for now sugar plantations lined the shores, called the "Sugar Coast," and New Orleans lay just ahead.

For the first time in many nights, Abe began to relax.

Finally it was their last night out. The next day they'd be in New Orleans—the queen city of the South.

"Let's tie up early tonight and get a good rest," Allen suggested. "We'll be mighty busy tomorrow."

They were just passing a big sugar plantation, so they poled to the bank and tied the boat fast. After a quick supper, they stretched out on the deck and went to sleep.

Hours passed, with no sound except the lap of water against the boat and the call of a whippoorwill.

Then came a stealthy rustle as a man cautiously crawled aboard. The sleeping boys did not hear.

Another man crept aboard, and another and another . . . seven brigands in all, making no sound except for the soft slap of their bare feet on the wooden deck. In the starlight their eyes glittered, evil and cruel. Crouching, ready to spring, they moved toward Abe and Allen.

Abe never remembered afterward what awakened him, but suddenly he was awake and staring

in horror at the dark figures coming at him. "Thieves! Thieves!" Abe yelled.

He sprang to his feet and grabbed for the nearest weapon—a stout crab-tree stick that Allen had used to push the boat away from the bank that morning. He swung it mightily and knocked one robber off the boat. There was a cry and a splash as the man hit the water.

Allen leaped to his feet, shouting, and striking out at his attackers. Suddenly the deck was a battleground of crashing fists and plunging bodies. Abe and Allen knew they were fighting for their lives. They were outnumbered, but they were strong, and Abe Lincoln—backwoods giant—towered over everybody as he thrashed out with his club.

A hard fist cracked Abe above the eye, but he hardly felt it. With a well-aimed blow of his club he knocked another robber into the water. The remaining brigands plunged overboard after their comrade. The crew of cutthroats made for the shore and disappeared like shadows among the trees.

Abe and Allen chased them a few steps up the

bank, then thought better of such foolish action.

"Let's cut loose and get out of here," Abe said. "They'll collect more of their gang and come back. Those thieves are mad now. They won't be beaten if they can help it."

Quickly they freed the boat and pushed out onto the dark water. Not until they were safe in mid-channel did they take time to examine their injuries. Both boys were battered and bruised. Abe had a bleeding cut above the right eye, and he tied a bandana over it.

"They meant to kill us," Allen said in a shaky voice. "They meant to steal our cargo and throw us to the fish. If you hadn't waked up, we'd be lying on the bottom of the river now."

Abe's face showed solemn agreement. "They wanted to kill us, that's certain," he said.

Through the rest of the night the flatboat swept down the mighty river toward New Orleans. Both boys were very much awake.

6. Back up the Rivers

New Orleans, Louisiana!

Abe had never seen a big city before, and he could scarcely wait to explore this colorful seaport of 40,000 people. It took the boys hours to nose their boat into the harbor, for the water was crowded with strange ships from all over the world.

"These boats are so thick that a fish couldn't swim through here without rubbing his scales off," Allen grumbled.

At last they found a place to dock, and Allen's good nature returned. He put on a nice suit he'd brought along and exchanged his moccasins for polished boots.

"I have to look prosperous when I go to sell the cargo," he laughed. "Then these merchants will think I know what's a fair price, and they won't try to offer me less."

Abe looked ruefully at his worn homespun shirt and buckskin trousers. "I reckon you'd better go alone, then. If they see me, they'll know right quick I'm a country boy. Anyway, I want to get started seeing the sights."

Allen went off on his chores. Abe settled his

coonskin cap on his head and went to explore the waterfront.

At once he found himself part of a strange and colorful throng. The wooden sidewalks were crowded with people unlike any Abe had ever seen. There were Dutch and French and Norwegian seamen, all speaking in languages he could not understand. There were Russians with blond mustaches, and Spaniards with knives in their belts and red silk handkerchiefs tied at their throats. A group of English sailors stood on a corner singing "O Fare-you-well, My Bonny

Young Girls." There were city men and women, dressed in fine clothing. Why, the women wore slippers or boots even though the weather was warm!

"I'm a long way from Gentryville," Abe told himself with a smile.

He prowled through stores filled with exotic wares. In one store he sniffed rich brown spices which had come all the way from India, and in another he ran one long finger over pieces of shimmering Chinese silk. In the marketplace he watched Negro slaves carry huge baskets of vegetables on their heads. Along the levee he counted more than a hundred deckhands rolling bales of cotton and barrels of sugar onto waiting ships.

When Allen returned, he brought good news. "I got more for the cargo than Pa expected, and the fellow who bought the flatboat—he wants the lumber to build a house—said we could keep the boat a couple of nights so we'll have a place to sleep while we're here. I told him we want to see New Orleans before we start home."

They went to a restaurant that Allen remembered from his earlier trip. The tables were set with white linen cloths and napkins, fine china, and expensive silverware. Abe looked at them with awe.

"This is a mighty fancy way to eat!" he declared.

Allen ordered shrimp gumbo.

"How do you like it?" he demanded as Abe sampled the new food.

Abe smacked his lips. "Best thing I ever ate," he said. Then he added loyally, "Except the squirrel stew that Mammy makes."

For two days they wandered through the busy, bustling city. "Looky yonder!" Abe kept saying. "Looky yonder!" Wherever they went, there were sights that fascinated him. He marveled at the handsome carriages that filled the streets. He admired the great houses with lacy iron balconies. Many houses were painted pink or lavender or yellow.

"First houses I ever saw that were painted to look like flowers," he told Allen.

Abe stood before a cathedral whose graceful spires lifted to the sky like praying hands, and he stared at its beauty until his eyes ached.

When he tiptoed to the door of the magnificent church, the music of an organ welled up in such a gush of melody that for a moment Abe thought sure it must be the angel choir his mammy sang about.

"Pa said we could ride a boat home or walk up the Natchez Trace," Allen announced on their last night in New Orleans. "I've been hearing bad things about the Trace. A lot of the trail goes through deep forests. It's dangerous. Men get robbed along it, and you know what I'm carrying." He patted his pocket.

"Let's go home by steamboat," Abe said. Allen agreed.

"I'll be glad when we get that money safe into your pa's hands," Abe said with feeling.

The next morning Abe waited at the gangplank to board the steamboat *Star of Dixie*. When Allen returned from arranging their fares, Abe asked, "What jobs did you get us? Do we carry cargo or hustle wood to the furnace?"

"Neither. Pa wouldn't want us to have to work for our passage. We've got a first-class cabin. We're going home in style." He handed Abe $24.

"Pa said I should pay you your money when we started home."

They went aboard the steamboat, and Abe quickly decided that the *Star of Dixie* must be as fine as the big houses he'd seen along the Sugar Coast. He rambled up and down steps, on this deck and that, looking at everything. On the main deck, roustabouts stacked freight and firemen tended the furnace. On the upper decks there were many handsome rooms with thick carpets and beautiful furniture. Wherever he looked, people were working to make the trip pleasant for the passengers. Waiters set tables. Maids made beds. In the kitchen, cooks roasted turkeys, pigeons, and wild ducks.

"It's a floating mansion!" Abe told Allen.

So back up the winding river they went, with Abe Lincoln enjoying luxuries he'd never known before. The boys soon became friends with the other passengers. Many of them were rich planters in crisp white suits who had made many trips on the Mississippi. Abe listened carefully as they told stories of the good times and the dangers of river travel.

"Ever hear of a catfish who can swallow a man in one gulp?" Abe asked a white-haired sugar planter one evening as they sat on deck.

"Is that a joke?"

Abe chuckled. "In a way. Still, there's a little fellow back home who'll be bound to ask me about it. He was worried I might get gulped."

The old gentleman smiled. "I remember now," he said in his courtly voice. "That must be the same fish I worried about when I was a boy. Well, here's what you tell your young friend.

"Once a farmer was shipping some hogs down river by steamboat," the old gentleman said, "and one hog died. The cook thought he'd save the dead hog for fish bait so he fastened it to a rope by means of a meat hook and dropped it overboard. Then he forgot it.

"When the passengers awoke next morning, they found they weren't going downstream but up! The boat was being carried stern foremost, upriver in spite of the engine. An enormous catfish had swallowed the bait and was hurrying home, towing the boat behind him."

Abe laughed. "That's the best fish yarn I've

heard yet. How did they get the boat free? Cut it loose?"

"The captain got out his rifle and shot the fish. Then the passengers ate catfish morning, noon, and night all the rest of the way to New Orleans!"

One morning Abe stood at a bow railing waving at a passing flatboat crew. Suddenly the huge, dripping branches of a dead tree began to rise from the water in front of the steamboat. Abe recognized the danger instantly.

"A sawyer ! A sawyer dead ahead!" Abe yelled. He knew that sawyers were trees washed into the river by floods. Their roots fastened in the riverbed while the branches rode the water. Depending on how the current ran, the branches could be sucked under the water or pushed above it. A boat moving in what looked like clear water might suddenly ram a sawyer that rose directly in front of it. The jagged branches could rip open the bottom of a boat the way a knife could split a pumpkin.

"A sawyer!" Abe yelled again and dropped to the deck as the *Star of Dixie* swerved sharply.

60

Overhead he could see the wet, black branches of the sawyer, like a great bony hand, reaching for the boat. The boat veered sharply again, there was a loud scraping noise, and the *Star of Dixie* skirted disaster with no more damage than some scratched paint.

"Abe! Abe! Are you all right?" Allen dashed up, panting. "Whew! When I saw you up here, and a branch of that sawyer right over your head, I thought sure it was going to knock you off the boat and under the paddlewheel!"

Abe's grin was a trifle crooked. "I'm still planning on getting home to Gentryville," he said.

Allen drew a deep breath. "Lucky you saw the sawyer and warned the pilot in time to turn the boat."

"I reckon," Abe said, but he knew that his real luck had been hearing the planters talk about sawyers only the night before.

Finally it was their last morning, and they were nearing Mr. James Gentry's wharf. The two boys stood on the main deck, waiting to dock. It had been almost three months since

they'd begun to build the flatboat. Now Abe had $24 to give to his pappy. He had a little scar over one eye. He'd seen a piece of the world. He'd kept his promise to Mr. Gentry.

"It's been a good trip, hasn't it, Abe!" Allen said.

"No two fellows ever had a better one," Abe agreed. "Tell your pa I'm grateful to him."

The boat docked at the empty wharf. No one had known they were coming, but there'd be plenty of welcoming later. Right now they were well pleased to slip quietly home to their families. For a moment they watched the *Star of Dixie* move away. From the deck some of the planters waved a friendly farewell.

Then the boys were alone. They shouldered their clothes bags.

"Good-bye, Abe."

"Good-bye, Allen."

Abe Lincoln hurried down the forest trail, a wide grin on his face. He had news—all sorts of news about the places he'd been and the things he'd seen—and he could scarcely wait to get home and tell it.

MEET THE AUTHOR

LaVere Anderson says she is "fascinated by southwestern history," and much of her writing for national magazines, newspapers, and for children reflects this interest. Years of experience as a teacher of creative writing at the University of Tulsa and as book editor of the *Tulsa World* prepared her for a career as an author. Mrs. Anderson, the mother of a son and two daughters, has conducted storytelling hours for children and story-writing classes for young teens at the Philbrook Art Center. She found working with youngsters such a "warmly rewarding experience" that she started writing stories especially for them.

MEET THE ARTIST

Cary studied at the Massachusetts College of Art before launching his career as an advertising artist. After ten years in the commercial field, he moved to his present home in West Barnstable, Massachusetts. Here, on beautiful Cape Cod, he does free-lance illustrations for publishers and advertising agencies. As a hobby, Cary paints, acts, and designs sets for the local drama club and goes fishing. Cary and his wife have three children "and all the usual excitements that go along with these."